Winston

O

Winston

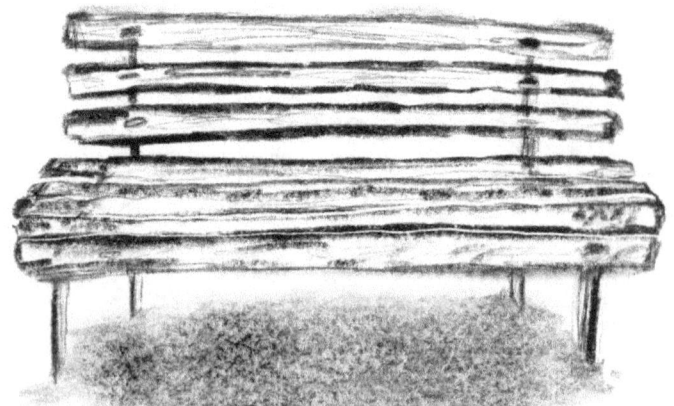

Rick Powell
WRITER

Marie Moldovan | Joe Mykut
EDITORS

O

Joseph Mykut -Editor

Marie Moldovan - Editor, Publication Layout, Illustration and Cover Design.

WINSTON

I Ain't Your Marionette Press, P.O BOX 184, Larder Lake ONTARIO, P0K 1L0, Canada.

ISBN: 978-1-998213-28-3

FOREWORD

Greetings, fellow literary travelers,

It is with great excitement and a touch of irony that I present to you "Winston," a mesmerizing narrative crafted by the ever-intriguing "Father of Mannequins," Rick Powell. As an editorial advisor for I Ain't Your Marionette Press, I've had the unique pleasure of diving into this dark and captivating tale.

Picture this: a rundown neighborhood where hope is as rare as a vinyl record in today's digital age. Here lives Julie, a young girl whose days are overshadowed by her mother's new boyfriend—a figure who brings more chaos than comfort. But, as fate would have it, Julie's life takes an unexpected turn.

On one of those seemingly endless, dreary walks home, she

crosses paths with Winston, an enigmatic old man whose presence is as captivating as it is mysterious.

Who is Winston? What secrets does he hold that could lift Julie from her adversity? Is he a savior, or a bringer of doom?

"Winston" is a tale of unexpected bonds and the profound impact they can have on our lives. As you flip through these pages, prepare to be drawn into a story where one encounter holds the promise of change.

Rick Powell's storytelling prowess shines through in this book, offering readers a journey filled with mystery and transformation. Trust me, "Winston" will resonate deeply with you, just as it has with me.

~Pita Black of Cranberree Ink

"Who knew the caws would be the toll my heart would pay for ending's bowl to ring the reaper for my will's collection?"

— Marie Moldovan,
20 Years of Winter.

The sea of autumn leaves rippled freely as he walked with a steady, tired gait. The day was as cloudy and overcast as the expression on his face. The whispering crunch of his scuffed shoes was the only sound as he made his way toward the old bench, apart from the bare branches overhead clacking and scraping—a language that only the season understands. He had been here before.

It was odd that the park district had placed a bench so far from the paved bike path that wound laboriously around the forest preserve on this edge of town. Perhaps some youths of questionable nature had placed it there. Or maybe it was positioned by the park district so walkers could rest and enjoy the lush forest all around: a momentary respite before they continued their walk back to their cars in the parking area hundreds of yards away.

Oddly, this was the only bench. This is where the story began, and this is where it will end.

Arriving at the bench, he sat down with a sigh. Both hands were buried deep in the pockets of his faded, long coat. His body seemed to meld into the bench, as if weighed down by the garment's thick leather. The cuffs of his trousers fluttered in the crisp air while he shifted to find a more comfortable position on the weathered wood. Without a hat, his curly white hair danced to the rhythm of the branches swaying above.

After clearing his throat and sniffing, he withdrew his right hand and delved into the inner left breast pocket of his coat. From it, he extracted a small, spiral notepad—its cover a gangrenous yellow, dog-eared from use. Digging deeper into the same pocket, he retrieved a pencil, its hue matching the notepad's aged cover.

"I'm tired," he wrote.

A stray leaf fell onto his chest, flattening against the white dress shirt he wore. Brushing it away with his hand, pencil still in his fingers, not even glancing at it, his eyes fixed on the notepad before him, he flipped the cover and scanned the pages before stopping at the center of one to see numerous names, indecipherable in his handwriting. Sniffing loudly, he crossed off one name and returned both pad and pencil to their place. Placing his hands back into his coat pockets, he sat there, looking forward.

Blowing in the wind were various debris—a paper wrapper here, a plastic grocery bag there. All of them flowed by like little beings at play. The man didn't notice. He only stared and thought again. *How long have I been doing this job?* Just a moment's rest, and he would be on his way.

Closing his eyes, he took a deep breath. If only he could stop thinking for a few minutes. Just not think about the next job.

***

She had walked this path so many times since they moved here three months ago, just to get out of that suffocating apartment.

Ever since her mom started dating Andy last year, they had had to move twice. *And for what? Because "Handy" Andy couldn't find a real job. No, not him. Just side jobs. Whatever he made, he just spent on booze and smokes anyway. The bastard. What did her mom see in him?*

A fast-food cup blew into her path. Crushing it under her loosely laced, weathered Nikes, she walked on, hands deep in the pockets of her grey hoodie. One knuckle was visible through the worn-out hole in the pocket, matching the frayed, random

4

holes in the blue jeans that covered her legs.

Frowning, she thought, *If Andy tries to get 'handy' with me, I'll scratch his eyes out.* She had seen the way he looked at her when her mom wasn't watching. She had tried to talk to her mom about it once and got slapped. If her dad were alive, he would never have hit her. She had cried all night about that. Sometimes, she hated her mother.

Walking on the cracked, black pavement, random leaves blew against her legs, a few crunching underfoot as she made her way around the bend.

Looking up at the branches overhead, their bony limbs clasped together like skeletal hands. She had taken this way before, from school, numerous times. Alone. Sometimes imagining herself as a forlorn princess in a fairy tale, waiting for her knight in shining armor to come galloping around the bend.

She remembered her dad reading to her in bed years ago. She loved those stories, and his voice always sounded so strong.

Wiping a tear that had started to flow down her cheek, she thought about him. Five years now. Five years and two of her mom's boyfriends later.

It's not fair, she thought as she wiped her flowing brown hair out of her face. In three more years, she would be eighteen. She would get a job and get as far away from this life as possible.

Making the turn, she saw the bench in the distance that she had passed numerous times before. *Odd*, she thought. Despite all the times she had walked this way, she had never seen anyone sitting there. It was so far from the pavement; she never thought anyone would use it.

God, I hope he's not a perv, she thought as she drew closer. She continued walking, giving him a sideways glance as she passed by. He was sitting there, hands in his pockets.

She felt a little nervous but relaxed momentarily as she saw his head lying back against the top of the bench, his eyes closed, the wind blowing the white curls of his hair, his face towards the cloudy, overcast sky.

She kept walking, quickening her step as she half-expected to hear the crunching of leaves behind her, imagining him running after her, grabbing her around the neck, and her scream—the loudest she would ever make in her life.

But the only sounds were her footsteps and the wind in her ears.

Slowing down, she thought,
*He's sleeping. He looks so old. So thin.
I could probably kick his ass if he
even tried anything.*

She turned her head quickly,
just to see him in the same spot. From
this angle, there was something odd
about his face. She thought she saw
him breathing. With a slight frown,
she continued walking at a steady
pace. *That coat looks too good for him
to be a bum.*

Dammit, she stopped.

***

Darkness. Just a few minutes
of darkness. Smelling the dead leaves
as they fell through the air, kissing
his cheek. Just a few more minutes.

He heard the crunching of
leaves but chose to ignore it. Whoever
or whatever it was would just pass him
by. Just leave him be. He had work to
do in a moment.

A few more minutes in his blessed darkness, just like at—

"Hey, Mister? You okay?" A young girl's voice. Lifting his head, he opened his heavy lids, looking at her without expression. A humble figure stood there, a few feet away, with her hands in her pockets—a vision of grey and blue, like the sky before a storm. He sensed her apprehension more than he saw it. Her hair was the color of the dead leaves falling around her, her eyes like those of a lost doe in a lonely field.

"Are you okay?"

Clearing his throat, he said, "Yes. Thank you for your concern. I am just taking a moment's rest. I have much to do, and today is one I haven't enjoyed in quite a while."

She seemed relieved to hear this. He noticed a relaxation in her demeanor as she heard his voice. Peering strangely at him for a moment, her head tilted just barely to the side, she said, "Oh, okay. It's just that I don't see people here much. I thought you might be sick or something."

She took a furtive step back, still looking into his eyes. "Well, take care," she said as she started to turn away.

"It is you who should be careful, young lady," he said, pointing to her feet with a thin finger. She looked down at the untied lace trailing in the leaves like a thin worm trying to hide.

How did he see that? She thought.

She looked at him again, into his eyes. *God,* she thought, *I've never seen eyes so weak and sad. So dark and so... tired.* So different from the gaze he gave her when she woke him; his voice was deep and strong. That voice brought back memories of a different face, a different time. She no longer felt scared. Even though his face failed to show any expression, she relaxed at that moment. She couldn't say why she did it, but she walked to the bench, far on the other side from him, and, bending down, began tying her lace.

"Thanks," she said quickly, not looking at him.

"You are most welcome," he said, with no emotion evident in his words.

God, she thought. *That voice. I've never heard anything like it. It scares and fascinates me at the same time.* Turning toward him, she said, "Well, I hope you have a good day. Are you sure you're going to be okay?"

"Yes," he said, looking down. "I have a job to do. My work is never done." He remained seated as the breeze blew past, not attempting to move.

A few seconds passed, and she said, "Oh, well, what do you do?" She put her hands back in her pockets and looked at him, her shoulders relaxing as she waited eagerly for his voice, looking at his face. The deep wrinkles and crevices were evident. Even though they were cast downwards, she tried to look into his eyes. For some reason, a sense of something flowed off him like some sort of aura. She couldn't pinpoint it.

"I give people... comfort," he muttered.

That's it, she thought. "Oh! So, you're a priest!" Relaxing, she bobbed her head in recognition. A slight smile crossed her lips.

He chuckled deep in his throat. "No, far from it. I just help people in their time of need." His position hadn't changed. There was a moment of silence, except for the sound of the branches fighting overhead. A crinkled cigarette pack wrapper tumbled to his worn shoe and lay there, like a dog's head on the lap of its master.

"My name is Julie," she said inquiringly. "What's yours?"

Reading the label of the wrapper on his shoe, the man whispered, "Winston."

Failing to see what he was looking at, still intent on the expressionless face and the sound of his voice, Julie found there was still something sadly fascinating about him. Her diminishing fear was replaced by curiosity. He seemed harmless.

God. I'm talking to a total stranger near the woods. Mom would freak, she thought.

A slight smile came to her lips.

"Ohhhhh..." she said. "Just like that Church guy we heard about in history class."

"Church?" His eyes looked up at her, questioningly. His brow furrowed, and a slight grin appeared at the edge of his mouth. He leaned forward as if preparing to stand.

"Ya know that England guy. He was a president or something. Always giving the peace sign," she said with a chuckle. She looked into his eyes and thought *she had never seen eyes so dark before. It's like I can see right into his skull.* She shivered for a moment at the thought.

"Oh yes, Churchill. He was a proud man. A strong man. I met him once." He rose, stretching his arms above his head, fingers extended as if reaching for the branches. The bones in his back and arms snapped, not unlike the snapping of the limbs overhead.

"Well," he continued, looking at her as he relaxed his frame, withered hands going back into his pockets, "It is time for me to go now. I have to get back to work. It was nice to meet you, Julie."

She didn't realize how tall he was. For a moment, it seemed that his whole body obscured the darkening forest behind him at the day's end. For some reason, she extended her small, pale hand out to him, just thinking how his hand would feel in hers. How could a tall, thin, tired man look so large at the same time?

"It was nice meeting you too, Winston," she said, waiting for him to grasp her hand. Her shoulders were set back, inadvertently trying to stand as tall as he. "I hope we meet again soon."

He looked down at her hand, with a slight look of apprehension on his face. He did not make any attempt to shake. He just looked up into her face with an emotion she couldn't recognize. Not a look of contempt or

disgust; it was almost like a slight...
fear?

Returning her hand to her pocket, she gave a slightly uncomfortable grin.

"Well. Take care," she said, backing up a few steps, about to turn around.

"Likewise to you, Julie," he responded with a slight nod.

Turning, she made her way through the leaves towards the paved path, walking a little more briskly than she cared to. As she reached the path, she turned around and saw him still standing there, like some forlorn scarecrow. She felt his gaze on her—a gaze that was not so much threatening as it was curious.

***

Walking up the concrete steps of the complex, Julie ran her hand along the chipped paint of the rail.

She could hear the arguing from as far away as across the street when she arrived. The passing cars could not drown out the shouts issuing from the second floor.

Opening the screen door, she closed her eyes for a moment before shouldering the heavy wooden door open. It had been sticking ever since they moved in, with Andy making no attempt to fix it. As she entered the small hallway adjacent to the equally sized kitchen, the shouting pierced her ears with its shrillness. All she could do was wince and try to walk as quickly as possible to avoid them.

Her mother and Andy were facing each other, arms waving wildly, resembling caricatures more than human beings. Andy was wearing faded jeans and a stained white t-shirt that did little to conceal his forming beer belly. His blond hair showed signs of receding, with more hair on the mullet at the back of his sweaty neck than on his brow.

Her mother was thinner than she should be for her age, the color of her faded, amateur tattoos matching the dark circles under her eyes. The rock t-shirt she wore had been Julie's until Andy spilled bleach on it—how, Julie would never know, as she had never seen him lift a towel to wipe anything. It looked too big on her mother's thinning frame, hanging on her just like her blond, unkempt hair that tossed around as she yelled with wildly gesticulating arms. "Well, you can't get a job if you don't get your sorry ass out there and start looking!" She heard her mother shout.

"Don't 'cha bitch at me! I've been fuckin' tryin'!" Andy screamed. Stopping, they turned their heads in unison to see Julie walking their way. They quickly gazed at her, then turned away in shame. Their waving arms, still looking tense, came down.

She turned to the left quickly and rushed down the hallway to her door, opening it just as she heard her mother's footsteps tramping up behind her.

"Julie, honey... wait."

Rushing into her room, Julie closed the door and pushed the button on the old, brass doorknob just as her mother began knocking.

"Julie? Open up. Everything's okay. We were just talking," her mother said softly, so Andy could not hear.

Ignoring her, Julie heard Andy's muted protests from the kitchen. After a minute, her mother exclaimed, "Damn it!" followed by the sound of her stomping back towards the kitchen to resume the "discussion" they were having when Julie first arrived.

Julie threw herself onto her unmade bed, the one she had left that morning. The afternoon light filtered through the old, gossamer bedsheet tacked up on the window frame, the white paint chipping and leaving specks on the floor. She looked at the door, hoping her mother wouldn't return to knock again. Pulling her legs underneath her, she moved closer to the head of the bed, the frame squeaking as it shifted further into the corner of the small room where it had been since they first moved in.

At the foot of the bed, against the wall, stood a wooden TV table adorned with a few dog-eared rock magazines from the thrift store down the street. Some of the covers had been torn off and tacked up sporadically in places on the wall above.

She lay there, looking at the pile of clothes in front of the small closet across from her, knowing she should get them washed but dreading the trip down to the laundry room.

On the front of the wooden door was the only photograph in the room—a four-by-seven picture tacked carefully in the center of the panel. It was a picture of a man in a blue work shirt, smiling into the camera. His short, brown hair was slightly ruffled by the breeze, as free flowing as the smile on his face.

His arms were raised, hands clasped around those of the little girl perched on his neck, her open-mouthed smile and head tilted to the side. Her curly hair, adorned with ribbons, formed a halo against the dreamy, blue sky and floating clouds behind her.

Looking at the picture, Julie closed her eyes, remembering better times, hoping the images behind her closed lids would blot out the muted arguing that tore through the thin walls.

A slight tear fell from her eye as she lay down, placing her head on the flat pillow and facing the wall, hoping against hope that she could sleep past dinner—if there was any— and wishing sleep would come quickly. *Maybe she wouldn't dream*, she thought. Waking up from one was always a disappointment, especially when it was a dream of a different world, a different life.

***

The morning found her at the bus terminal across from the complex, the clouds smothering the sun as it vainly tried to fight through them. She had been awakened by Andy's snoring through the closed bedroom door he shared with her mom, the sound reverberating off the walls as she quickly got ready for school. Her mother was absent, already at work at the corner diner where she worked five days a week. That job, along with the last of the insurance money left from when her father died at the electrical plant, was all they had to survive on these days.

The inheritance money was almost gone, dwindling over the last few months with all the moving they had done. She had found a glass pipe and rolling papers in her mother's drawer two weeks ago while searching for clean socks, so she could guess why the money was going quicker than it should. She didn't even want to attempt to confront her mom about it; just thinking about it filled Julie with increasing disgust.

She stood there with her hood up, trying in vain to warm the chill creeping down the nape of her neck. With her back turned to the few other girls in the terminal, she tried to blot out their giggling and trivial conversations about boyfriends and drama, all while looking down the street, hoping for a glimpse of the bus so she could finally sit down and find some warmth before it took her to the mundane structure of the high school she dreaded.

The street was filled with passing cars of commuters going to their jobs, and routine destinations stretched out in either direction— strip malls, auto repair shops, and fast-food places. A few pedestrians wandered here and there, walking around like lost children.

About a hundred yards down the street, Julie saw a dark form in a black coat exit from under the awning of Hwang's Chinese Restaurant and walk away from her. His curly, white hair moved in the breeze of the passing cars, the dark figure growing smaller and smaller as he lumbered away. As the hulking form of the commuter bus came into her line of vision, she lost sight of him.

Was that Winston? she thought to herself as she clumped her way quickly up the steps of the bus.

She rushed to the back as it pulled onward, wishing the public transport had windows in the back so she could see if the form remained in sight. Sitting hard with a sigh, she began to think. What would he be doing out here? She had gotten food from that place a few times when they first moved here, but she never knew they would be open this early. Maybe he knows the owner. Vaguely, she remembered the elderly owner and his wife. They were short and always smiling. Maybe Winston worked on this stretch of town? That would be cool. *She should ask him if she saw him again,* she thought with a grin. Besides, the day wasn't too bad for a walk home. Maybe take the path by those woods again.

The bus moved on, blending in with the traffic. If there had been

windows in the back of the bus, Julie
would have seen the flashing, colored
lights of the ambulance as it turned
into the parking lot of the restaurant;
an old, squat woman with an apron
running out from under the awning,
waving her arms wildly to it as it
turned in.

***

In the brisk air of late
afternoon, she decided to forsake the
ride home the bus usually took as it
made the two-mile stop-and-go
journey back to the apartments. She
was in no hurry to get home anyway.
She had been late for dinner before,
but at the pace she was walking, she
could still get there in no time.
Besides, the forest preserve ran right
along the highway halfway home, and
she could cut through there and see if
anyone waited at the bench. She knew
the idea was a foolish one since she
only met him once. Hell, she might not

see him again, but just the way she felt in those few moments with him was a welcome change to the time she had lived here.

As she took the familiar curve around that bend, she spied the bench, empty. The only occupants were a few scattering leaves. Sighing, she walked on, feeling not so much disappointed as foolish. She continued down the bike path and, after a hundred yards or so, turned off and weaved in and out between the trees, towards the sounds of the cars on the highway just ahead. This way, she could walk down the side of the highway and pass the shops and stores lining the street as she went home, which was several blocks away.

As she passed Hwang's, she saw a white poster board haphazardly taped to the inside of the door. The white sign was a strong contrast to the dark interior. No evidence of anyone in there. Just the abandoned booths in the window.

She ran up under the awning in front of the sign. As if written in a hurried hand, "CLOSED UNTIL FURTHER NOTICE," showed in black marker. She cupped her hands on her brow as she placed her face up to the window in a vain attempt to peer in. Nothing.

Stepping back, she began the long jog towards the apartments up ahead. She knew that Winston was leaving there this morning. *Did they close up? He said he helped people. How does he help someone by closing up their business? Is he some sort of loan officer? A city worker, perhaps? They were nice people, too.*

As she ran up the steps of the apartment complex and pushed open the door, she saw Andy sitting at the kitchen table. A couple of beer cans were on the table surrounding a half-eaten pizza on a pan in the center. Her mother stood with her back turned to her at the sink, still in her waitress uniform as she washed a few soiled plates before putting them in the rack. An aroma of pepperoni in the air mingled with cigarette smoke as it trailed from the partially filled ashtray next to the pizza.

"You're late," her mother mumbled as Andy turned his head to look at her.

"I'm sorry. I missed the bus," Julie said as she closed the door. Andy took a swig from one of the cans and, containing a belch with a smirk under his stern look, said, "You seem to miss that bus a lot. You don't wanna go and worry your mom like that, kid."

"Sorry," she mumbled as she turned to take off her hoodie and hang it on the hook on the wall behind the door. She rubbed her bare arms at the chill she felt in the hallway.

She felt more of a chill as she walked up to the table to grab a slice of the lukewarm pizza, trying to avert her gaze from Andy as he looked at her. She went to the cupboard near her mother to grab a paper plate as her mother said, "How was school?"

Her mother did not even turn her head to acknowledge Julie as she continued to rinse the dish.

"Eh, ok," she said as she sat across from Andy at the small table and started eating. "I passed by Hwang's on the way home. Why did they close up?" she asked between chews.

"The owner died today," Andy said as he picked up the half-crushed cigarette pack on the table and sat back in the chair, searching in the breast pocket of his plaid flannel shirt for his lighter. "I ran into

Charlie in apartment 2-E. He told me that the owner had a heart attack this morning. Charlie's sister works at the dry cleaners across from the restaurant and saw the ambulance take him out and everything."

Julie coughed up a piece of pizza in shock. "W-what?" She said, her eyes watering as she continued coughing and managing to get the coughs under control as she grabbed one of the many napkins scattered on the table.

"Yeah," he said, digging a cigarette out of the pack. "He had a big ol' grabber while he and his wife were doing the morning prep. The old woman did what she could, but it must've been quick. Hell, it was only the two of them running the place. Guess it won't be opening for a while."

Looking wild-eyed at Andy, Julie exclaimed, "Was anyone else there? God! The poor man! He seemed so nice." She turned her head up to her mom, who was starting to clear the napkins and beer cans from the table, a shocked expression still on her face. "Did you hear anything today?"

"No, I was too busy working to get food on the table today to go visit any friends," her mother replied in a cold tone.

As Julie saw her mother's profile, she noticed the dark blue-like bruise on her cheekbone on the left side of her face. "Mom! God! What happened?" Julie asked.

Andy returned her mother's cold look. "Your mom has got to be careful at work. She knows how slippery those floors are when they're mopping in the morning. She has got to be more careful," he said, more as a statement to her mother than an answer to Julie.

"I'll be okay. I just gotta watch where I'm going with things. I'm fine," Julie's mother said as she looked away and threw out the napkins and cans into the garbage. Julie turned her head to Andy and narrowed her eyes in a speechless glare. Andy just looked into her eyes with a smirk.

"It's a good thing I ran into Charlie. I got a delivery job from him to do for the next few weeks until I get something else. Good money. Can't say no to that," he said. His voice was raised as if directing it to her mother, who had finished cleaning up and left the kitchen. They were both looking into each other's eyes. No sound in the kitchen as they heard her mother's bedroom door close with a click.

"I swear to God if you..." Julie began in a harsh whisper but was instantly interrupted by the sound of his chair scraping the linoleum as he stood with a cough. His gaze did not leave hers.

"Well, I'm going to get an ice pack for your mom and something that will help with the pain," he said with a chuckle, interrupting her. "You can finish cleaning up, can't you? You should start to catch that bus more often from now on. So we can all eat together more. Like a family."

Extinguishing the cigarette in the ashtray, he sauntered away and went down the short hallway to the bathroom. Julie placed both hands palm-down on the table as though about to push herself up but was frozen in place, staring at the tabletop as she heard the medicine cabinet open; Andy whistling a nameless tune.

Julie remained in that same position, her heart beating as if to pounce, as he left the bathroom and walked down the hallway into her mother's room.

That bastard, she thought. *Did he hit her mother, or was he making her think he did so he could play some sort of sick game? First, the news about the old man, and now this!* She tried to process the last fifteen minutes since she got home. *God, I cannot believe this*, she stood up with a jolt.

Stomping down the hallway to her room, she stood in front of her mother's door, adjacent to her own. Staring at it, wanting to pound on the door but hearing the muted murmurs of them talking caused her to hesitate. *Why would she even bother?* Julie thought. *Andy would just be all comforting and nice. He would be Mr. Prince Charming for a few days until the next argument, and it would just repeat. Repeat and repeat. Julie lost count of the arguments she had had with her mother about him. God,* she thought, *what's the point?*

Abruptly turning, Julie returned to the kitchen, grabbed her hoodie, and rushed out the door. She thought *they could clean up their mess* as she hurried down the stairs. Twilight was fast approaching as she reached the curb and started walking down the sidewalk toward the other side of town. She wished she could just get lost, even though she had walked these same streets so many times in the past few months. The frustration and anger were the only feelings keeping her warm as the night grew chilly and brisk.

The streetlights were coming on as she continued walking on the cracked sidewalk, past the myriad of shops that were closing for the night and the larger brick edifices, long since abandoned, that eclipsed them. The emptiness of the dark windows she saw mirrored the emptiness of her soul.

No matter how many times she left that apartment, she would always have to end up going back there. Feeling like an invisible leash was pulling her in. She walked faster and more determined just to feel some sense of freedom as the night approached.

***

Her feet were sore after walking for the last few hours; she hadn't been paying attention to where she was going, just passing under the streetlights and looking down at her elongated shadow as it stretched forward away from her. A little relief crept into her mind as her thoughts of the apartment diminished the farther she went.

As the night wore on, a light mist caressed her face with the threat of fog. She didn't know the time, and she didn't care. The cars passing by were oblivious to her hooded form as it lumbered on.

Up ahead, a few blocks distant, she saw the largest building in her sight, lit by the many lampposts surrounding the structure, reflecting off the hoods of a multitude of adjacent cars. A few cars were turning into it as she approached for a closer look. She had never been this far before.

She saw the blue weathered sign with the white "H" in the center on the lamppost ahead of her and realized that she was coming up to the community hospital. *Maybe I could become a nurse someday*, she thought. It would be good to do something to help someone. Maybe she could get a job here cleaning or something when she grew older. It would be a good experience, and she wouldn't have to be home so much.

She remembered when her father was in the hospital and how nice the nurses had been there. Her step slowed as she remembered with a frown. She turned her head as she passed the columned portico of the glass-enclosed area where numerous people were going in and out of the large revolving doors that swished open into the night. The 'Out-Patient' sign was barely discernible as some people were pushed out in wheelchairs to waiting cars by women in white; others walked arm-in-arm with elderly individuals to the waiting vehicles.

As she drew closer, she saw to the right of the doors, barely visible in the shadow of the portico, a familiar dark-coated figure. He was jotting something down on a pad of paper. She let out a small gasp and walked quickly toward him, swerving around the waiting cars, their headlights like misty beams in the night as a small fog settled slowly into the darkness.

"Winston!" she called out. A small grin appeared on her face. He looked up at her in mild shock, then watched her with narrowed eyes that soon relaxed with her approach. He slowly put the pad and pencil in his breast pocket and straightened his thin frame, putting his hands in his coat pockets as he greeted her with a nod.

"Good evening, dear Julie," he said with a slight smile, his voice even more odd in the night. "What is a young girl doing out on a night like this? You should be at home. A heavy fog will soon be approaching."

"Trust me," she said. "I feel a thousand times safer here than at home. God. This is so cool! I was just wondering when I could see you again. This is an amazing coincidence. Do you work at the hospital? Are you a doctor?" she asked with enthusiasm.

"A doctor? No... No. Just another person I had to... help. Another individual I had to talk to. To settle some affairs. That is part of my job. I just go where I am sent. So, tell me, child, what brings you here on a night like this?" he asked again, his tone somber.

"I just had to go for a walk. Try to think and get away from things. A lot of home drama and stuff. Sometimes, a person just has to get away and clear their head, you know?" She said as she looked up at him. "I'm so glad I ran into you. I saw you coming out of Hwang's restaurant this morning. Did you know the owner died today?"

"I do not know about this restaurant called Hwang's," he said, looking into her eyes.

Julie paused for a moment; the only sound was the slamming of the last remaining car doors behind her. The night seemed darker now, and she could only make out the white of his hair and the shirt underneath his jacket. A small chill went through her body, and she thought she was glad she couldn't see his gaze. Was it the tone of his voice, which had become somewhat darker, or just the feeling of being near a hospital again?

"Oh, uh, sorry... It looked like you from a distance. I could've been wrong. I'm not that awake in the morning. Hell, I'm not that awake most of the time," she said with a forced chuckle, her hands deep in the pockets of her hoodie as she tried to warm herself from the cold.

"Let me walk you home, Julie. This night will make you ill. It isn't proper for you to be out like this. Please, lead the way," he said. As he stepped away from the wall, she was relieved to see that his eyes were not as dark as she had imagined. He still looked extremely tired, just like before.

"Sure," she said, cocking her head, "Just this way." Even though the thought of going back home didn't appeal to her, at least she would be walking with someone, and she would be away from the hospital. She didn't even know this man, and now she was walking home alone with him. Why didn't she feel afraid or even a little bit wary? She couldn't explain it. She just somehow trusted him not to harm her.

She had known Andy for a few months and was scared to be in the same room with him, but she had just met this man twice, hadn't spoken more than a few words, and now she was walking alone into the night with him. *I am so screwed up*, she thought.

As they walked away from the hospital and across the road to the other side of the street, Julie kept her gaze downward. His shadow now accompanied hers under the glare of the streetlights. She deliberately slowed her pace, not so much for his sake but to delay the return to the apartment she dreaded. A thought struck her, and she glanced at him sideways. "Don't you have a car? There are still a few buses that run this late if you want to take one," she said, her voice tinged with uncertainty about the long walk home.

"No, the night is quiet. My work is done for now. I do not need a car. I will walk with you to ensure you get home safely, then I will be on my way. Time passes quickly when you have company," he replied, his voice punctuated by a cough.

She chuckled, trying to lighten the mood. "You seem exhausted, and I just want to make sure 'the night

44

does not make you ill,'" she mimicked his earlier concern.

"It seems I have been exhausted for a long time, longer than I can remember," he said, his tone flat, either missing her humor or choosing to ignore it.

Julie felt a moment of awkwardness as they continued walking, the sound of their footsteps the only accompaniment. "Can't you take a vacation or something? Get some rest? You can't work all the time. Hell, I wish my mom's so-called 'boyfriend' would get a job. He is such a lazy fuck...oops!" She quickly covered her mouth, a slight smile betraying her amusement. His expression remained unchanged. "Sorry," she added.

"Do not apologize, child," he said, his gaze still fixed on the ground. "You are only speaking what's in your heart. Never be sorry for speaking your truth. There are more truths in this world than you can imagine, and more lies than you can ever conceive."

She laughed, shaking her head. "Wow, aren't you a Debbie Downer? You really do need a vacation. I thought I was the gloomy one. Dude, you gotta lighten up. Life is too short."

"You have no idea, my child," he said, looking up at her. Noticing her frown, he cleared his throat and changed the subject. "Tell me about this boyfriend of your mother's. He does not sound like a pleasant individual."

"Not much to say," she shrugged. "He was okay when my mom first met him. Now, he's just a jerk. My mom feels like she needs a man around, I guess. Ever since my dad..." She paused, swallowing hard. "It's been tough. She just works and hangs

46

out with Andy. It's like she doesn't even see me anymore." She rubbed her eyes, the mist making them water.

"May I ask what happened to your father?" he inquired, his voice carrying a note of genuine concern.

Julie looked ahead, lost in thought. "There was an accident at the electrical plant where he worked. Electrocution. They said he wasn't following 'Proper Safety Procedures.' It's bullshit. He was still breathing when they brought him to the hospital. He died right after Mom, and I got there. He was always so careful. He took care of everything, including us. I just wish I could've said goodbye, heard his voice one more time." She hugged herself tightly, feeling the cold more acutely, her damp hair sticking out, hiding her face from view.

"I am sorry, child," he said softly. "Do not worry. I am sure his last thoughts were of you. The pain may not leave, but in time, it becomes easier to bear. Such events are hard, especially for someone as young as you were. You have many questions, I'm sure. I wish I had the answers to ease your soul."

"Thanks," she replied, giving him a small smile. For a moment, it seemed he smiled back.

"You are a strange man, Winston. I don't know anything about you, yet here I am, telling you my life story. You won't tell me what you do, you have no car, and you look like you've been wearing those clothes forever. Why all the mystery? Tell me about yourself for once," she asked, her curiosity piqued. She felt odd being so forward with him, but somehow, she thought he would not be offended.

"I am just, as you might say, a loner. I am not used to being in the presence of people too much. I am accustomed to keeping a lot to myself. It is hard for me to explain and probably much harder for you to understand," he said.

Julie thought for a moment, looking at their shadows. "I think I understand more than you think," she replied. "I know how you feel." A somber expression crossed her face as they continued walking. They shared no other words in the mist. They both felt the night envelop them, content in each other's company. Sometimes, there is no language you can put to that. A couple of cars drove by, oblivious to both of them; their headlights vainly piercing the fog as they passed.

***

Julie entered the apartment. Two things hit her senses as she walked in. One was the muted sound of laughter from her mother's bedroom, barely discernible in the kitchen as she entered, the only light on was the one above the dirty stovetop. The other was the familiar smell of marijuana wafting through the hallway as she went to her room.

Well, I guess that's one of the fringe benefits of his 'delivery' job, Julie thought as she slammed her door. *I guess Mom forgave him. She knew Andy had hit her. All that talk about her co-workers being so careless. What a lying dick,* she thought angrily. The only sound she heard as she fell onto the bed was the failed attempt at muted laughter from across her room.

The night had finished so calmly, too. Winston was so nice. They had barely said anything else on the way home. She was a little embarrassed by opening up to him, and she guessed that was why he didn't say much afterward. She probably made him feel awkward.

She wanted to know more about him, but part of her still did not want to ask too much. It wasn't for the fact of prying into the personal life of a total stranger. It was more like not wanting to have the mystery about him revealed. She thought she would find out that all he was, was some boring counselor who was just trying to be kind to a girl he thought was from a troubled home, and eventually, he would refer her to some place for help or the Department for Children and Family Services, and then it would be back to the same old boring life again. Just with more added drama.

She had already heard about all that stuff in school. *Troubled teens. Go here. Go there. Talk to blah-blah-blah.*

Maybe she should talk to someone. Maybe she shouldn't be scared of Andy. He was more pathetic than intimidating. She felt a little sorry for him, even though she despised him. Maybe she would give it a few days, and then when she ran into Winston again, she would talk to him about it.

She thought she should get up and take a shower. They will pass out soon, but she was tired from the long walk tonight, and she could always get up early to take one.

She looked across the room at the picture on the door. She thought her dad would have liked Winston. It must have been the eyes. Sometimes Winston's eyes could look as comforting as her father's, and other times they looked so dark she could hardly describe them. She had made him smile a few times. She grinned when she thought about it. *Maybe I was breaking through his mysterious exterior,* she wondered.

Julie got up, went to her closet, and kicked away the dirty clothes still in front of her door. *I am going to do laundry tomorrow*, she thought as she opened the closet, took her pajamas off the plastic hanger, changed into them, turned off the light, and got into bed. As soon as her head hit the pillow, she felt herself dozing off, and before the darkness of sleep overcame her, she thought that there was finally something to look forward to tomorrow—a new day and hopefully a new chance to see her new friend again.

Night is the time when most children drift off to slumber, experiencing visions that we, as adults, lose as we age. The night should be for rest, to put aside any deeds and disillusionments that have haunted us during the day—a time to gather strength for the following day, which can be filled with new promises and a chance to offer the world what we haven't given the day before.

More often than not, the night can also bring out people and things that, by the light of day, mercifully, our eyes never see.

Julie was curled up in slumber, probably the most at rest she had been in weeks. She did not hear the door, which she had failed to lock, open. She did not feel the bed shift as a dark form sat upon it.

She barely felt being turned over onto her back.

What she did feel, before any dreams she had turned into a nightmare from which she could not escape, were two things:

The heavy, clammy hand that covered her mouth.

The hot, stinging burn of the collar of her pajama top scraping the back of her neck as the garment covering her chest, which just moments ago was as warm as her softly beating heart, was ripped open.

54

Night. Some acts are so indescribable to the human mind that to put them into words would shine a light onto something that cannot be comprehended. When it happens to a woman or a child, it is something beyond anything anyone can fathom.

***

The leaves were more active than usual that morning as Winston walked the familiar cracked blacktop on the bike path. He was feeling something indescribable.

It was not the last two jobs; they were just like all the others he had done before. He should have felt some relief that they went so easily. For a long time, the mundane process of completing each task was on the edge of discomfort, bordering on pain—if that was the proper way to describe it.

There was no pain in what he did, just the momentary feeling of nothingness that draped over him when he was done. One would think after so long, he would become somewhat immune to it, that it would not even faze him, that it would be a grain of sand on an endless beach or a speck of quiet dust on an old, abandoned structure that has been untenanted for ages.

Meaningless.

For some reason, he had a feeling of expectation that today would be different from any other. It took him a few moments as he walked to realize one thing that was different about today.

The fatigue that had hung over him like a cloak of lead for so long was gone.

This was the day. It had finally happened. There was one time per millennium that this occurred.

He had seen so many of his other jobs feel this way before he had led them in the direction they had to go. Of course, there were times when many had argued, pleaded, and begged not to go. More often than not, others just accepted that they had to go in the direction he directed them to. It was not his place to make that choice; it was just his job.

He had empathized with most of them, even feigned sympathy for more. After doing this for so long, one tends to forget how to use emotions. When you do feel them, they are like the return of something you lost a long time ago, something you don't realize you lost, and after having gained it back, you look at it strangely and wonder how you could have had it in the first place.

His step was more energized as he started walking around the familiar bend. The leaves that blew around him were like little playful creatures that wanted to reveal a secret but were waiting for the right moment. The little whispers they made as they scraped the ground and each other held his attention as he saw the bench come into his line of vision as he made the final turn.

At first, all he saw was the bench and the area surrounding it, covered with a multitude of brown and golden leaves. The limbs above swayed freely, as if happy to be without the burden of so many below. The center of the bench seemed higher than the piles of leaves on either side. He paused as he noticed something else, something that made him stop in his tracks.

The movement of that pile had more to do with the shivering body underneath it than the cold air swirling around him as he walked toward it. As he got closer, he saw the familiar grey and blue clothing of the trembling form as it lay on its side, curled into itself, barely having enough room on the aged wood that held it.

Winston knelt before the bench and started brushing the dead leaves off her as he looked at the hood she had pulled over her face. He let out a small gasp as he saw the moistness of her cheek and the bridge of her nose as tears ran like rivulets down them.

"Julie?" he whispered, brushing the matted hair away from her face, noticing the blood-clotted, bitten lip and purplish bruise on the side of her jaw. "Child, what has happened?"

"W-W-Winston?" she asked, never opening her eyes or attempting to sit up. Her knees were pulled up to her chest, concealing her arms as she hugged her midsection. The old bench vibrated with the motion of her constantly trembling form. "Is i-i-it you?" she muttered.

"Yes! Yes! It is me, my child," he whispered, louder than he should have, afraid of frightening her. "Tell me what has happened?!"

"Andy...he...he...last night. Oh God...it hurts! It hurts so much. I'm bleeding. I can't go back. I can't go back. Help me...help me...please," she said, attempting to open her eyes to look at him.

"Alright, child...alright. Let me help you up. We will get you to a hospital and notify the authorities," he said as he tried to help her sit up.

"No! No! No police. No hospital. He said if I told anybody, if I told my mom, he would hurt her. He would do worse. He would...he would... Oh god oh god..." she sobbed uncontrollably.

Winston closed his eyes. This was not supposed to be, he thought. The time cannot be now. It cannot be her.

"Julie," he whispered, "you cannot let him have that power over you. You have to make him pay for this terrible thing he has done to you. You have to..."

Julie's eyes opened wide, bloodshot and pleading as she looked at him. "No, no, no, no... my life will be worse. I want to get away. I don't want to be here. My mom... I know how she is. I've seen the drugs. It'll make things worse. She will just use more. We have no money. Lawyers. Doctors. She can't do this. I can't do this. I want to go away. I don't want this life anymore. I want my Daddy. Oh, God! I want my Daddy!" She started wailing, wincing at the pain as she clutched herself tighter.

He looked at her and tried again to pull her up, but she winced and let out a small shriek. He sighed and looked up into the trees; the dry branches clacked together as if

telling him something he did not want
to hear.

"You help people. You comfort
people. I have nowhere else to go.
Take me away from here. Please. God.
Please... I don't want this anymore..."
she looked at him. Her voice now went
into a whisper. His gaze looked down
into her eyes. He saw the innocence
lost that would never come again. Eyes
that he had seen so many times
before. He knew by that lost look that
if he did not do something, she would
do something to move on to that other
place herself.

His place.

She quietly sobbed and hitched
as the leaves fell on and around her.

"Child, it is not your time for
me to take you away from here to
anywhere else your journey lies," he
said, his voice trembling slightly. His
shaking hand inadvertently touched

the breast pocket where the pad and pencil were.

"There is only one thing I can do. The last thing for me to do," he continued, his eyes distant. "I knew this time was coming. Just like it has happened to others before me and before them."

He took a deep breath, steadying himself. "I will be moving on to my rightful place. A dark place that I knew about but only had glimpses of all this endless time doing what my job required me to do."

"You do not understand what I am saying, but you will in time," he said softly, a hint of sadness in his voice. "I do not make the rules. I just follow them. I follow them just like the countless others before me."

He stroked her hair as she looked at him, both of their eyes glued to each other's. He moved his mouth to her ear and whispered, "You will be free of everything that is now and that is behind in the past, but you will be damned in a way that you cannot comprehend. I cannot erase the memory, but I can take away the pain you are feeling. You have to be sure of the choice you make, my child."

She felt his dry, thin hand. So different from the hands of the beast hours before. She shivered at the touch. The shiver was not from fear but the extreme coldness she felt through her hair and with every fiber of her being. A cold that made her forget the pain for a second. A cold that eclipsed the wind as it blew around their forms alone at this edge of the forest.

A tear rolled over the bridge of her nose and dropped to the dry wood of the bench as she looked at him in an unblinking stare and said, "I don't want this anymore. I want to be damned. I do not care. I don't want this anymore... please."

He looked at her with a look of utter despair. A single tear fell down his cheek.

"Take my hand, Child," is all he said.

The wind stopped for a moment. The multitude of branches up above stopped their waving and dry sounds they were making and hung motionless as if mourning the passing of something that only the elements can understand.

The dark clouds overhead rolled at their silent pace as if not wanting to disturb the only two figures in their sight far below. Two statue-like figures.

One figure, dark and kneeling, head down in supplication, clasping the hand of another, covered with leaves, lying on its side on the aged wood of the bench. Both of their forms were still as stone.

***

I hate this beat, Officer Cartwright thought as he walked along the snow-dusted path that wound around the preserve. He was grateful this town had experienced a light winter so far. The first snow of February wasn't too bad—only a few inches.

Ever since he moved to this town in November, it had been one shift-change after another. Police force cutbacks, shrinking budgets, the problems never seemed to end. He sighed, kicking a snowball off the path. To top it all off, the economy in this low-income town had seen its fair share of domestic abuse claims, drug peddling, and a rise in vagrancy throughout the town and neighboring cities.

As if to add insult to injury, his sergeant had reassigned him from the night shift to patrolling the preserves, looking for any homeless who had been ousted from the streets elsewhere. He adjusted his hat against the cold wind. Fortunately, last month he had only encountered a few piss-reeking winos to shoo away.

As he lumbered around the bend, panting, he thought he shouldn't complain. His wife had mentioned he needed to exercise more (the doctor had warned him that his cholesterol would be the death of him), but he would be on break soon after this one last walk-through. As he rounded the bend, he spotted a coated figure on the snow-covered bench.

Goddammit, he thought, can't they fucking just go somewhere else?

Hey, you," he shouted, "This preserve is closed! Get the hell outta here!" He waved his arm towards the figure as it stood and started walking his way. He noticed that it was a teenage girl in a coat dragging along the snow as she trudged towards him.

Just great, he thought, *a druggie or runaway. I am in no mood for writing a report. Too cold and starving.*

"Kid, come here. What the hell are you doing out here?" he asked sternly, spittle coming out from his lips mixing with the mist of the chilly air.

"Sorry officer, just had to cut through and took a rest for a minute. Going to work," she said.

He looked at her disheveled hair and tired eyes. "Empty those pockets and show me what you have. You have I.D.?"

She put her hand in her pocket, and he put his to his holster momentarily as she pulled out a small pad and pencil and handed it out to him. He just stopped and looked into her sad, tired eyes and felt a moment of pity for her.

Another homeless kid, he thought. "Listen, just get a move on. You can't be here," he said, not attempting to take the pad of paper. Something about her voice was odd, somehow. It scared him for a moment. She probably had a cold or something. He didn't want to deal with this now.

"Thank you," she said. "I have a lot to do today." *Her expression did not change. It's like she has no emotion. Most kids get frightened when I come up to them,* he thought. *Creepy kid.*

She started to walk down the path in the opposite direction as he watched her go.

"Get yourself home, kid. Wherever that is. You'll catch your death out here!" he yelled at her as she shuffled away.

The girl just turned back and gave him a look that he could not describe, then she continued walking away as the snow started to gently fall. Officer Cartwright turned around with a sigh as he went back to where he came from, eager to go to his patrol car and the warmth the heat inside would bring as he left.

The snow became heavier as it fell, obliterating any evidence of footsteps from either individual and covering the mark of the aged coat that it left on the bench as if it wasn't even there, to begin with.

DEATH

WHY DO YOU FEAR ME?
I AM YOUR FRIEND.
I BUT GUIDE TRAV'LERS
ROUNDING THE BEND —
LEAD THEM TO FREEDOM
FROM TIME AND AGE,
HELP THEM START
WRITING A NEW PAGE...

SEEK FOR ME NEVER,
KEEP YOUR COURSE TRUE —
WHEN I AM NEEDED
I'LL COME TO YOU,
THEN I WILL SHOW YOU
ROADS WITHOUT END —
WHY DO YOU FEAR ME?
I AM YOUR FRIEND.

~CLARENCE E. FLYNN

ACKNOWLEDGEMENTS

In the cringy corridors of creation, I owe my deepest gratitude to those who stood by me amidst the chaos.

To my family, your unwavering support has been the beacon in the shadows guiding me through the abyss.

To my editors, your sharp eye and relentless pursuit of perfection have breathed life into this tale of despair, unearthing the horrors that lurk within.

To my friends and beta readers, your honest critiques and

steadfast encouragement have been the pillars of this journey, standing firm against the encroaching darkness.

And to you, the reader, for daring to traverse this dystopian landscape with me. Your courage and curiosity are the lifeblood of this story, illuminating the shadows and confronting the terrors that lie in wait.

~Rick Powell

ABOUT THE AUTHOR

Rick Powell

Rick Powell is a resident of Oak Forest, Illinois, U.S.A. Rick began writing horror and dark fiction in 2012. His poetic and narrative talents have graced the pages of various publications, including Infernal Ink Magazine and the tantalizing anthology Lustcraftian Horrors: Erotic Stories Inspired by H.P. Lovecraft.

ABOUT THE EDITORS

Joseph Mykut

Joseph Mykut is a native of Alabama. They are an author, artist, illustrator, editor, photographer, and agent. Their artwork and photography are on display internationally in Ontario, Canada and can be found in the anthologies *3 Amigos Ink and*

Splatter Lonely Soul in the Darkness, The Way of the Crow and Shattered Psyche. All anthologies are **I Ain't Your Marionette Press** publications out of Canada. They also authored and illustrated the children's book, "Beautiful Boy", of the same publishing house.

Joseph's art and photography uniquely focuses on the random, seemingly unimportant aspects of the everyday environment surrounding us. They hope this draws attention to the deeper details that express the magic and beauty in the otherwise mundane.

As a member of the LGBTQ2+ community as well as walking the path of Shamanism, they hope to create and represent a more tangible bridge between the physical life experience and the world beyond our physical senses.

Joseph was born and raised in the deep south of the United Sates in what's known as the bible belt. His influences have developed over time to be more of the universe and of spirituality rather than religion.

However, Joseph is an ordained minister with the Universal Life Church as it aligns with his perspective that there is truth found in all religious beliefs as they are all smaller pieces to a greater picture.

They identify as a two spirited being or even multi spirited being and identify with all ideas of the gender spectrum. They believe in the existence of both light and dark or positive and negative energies leaving the truth of who we are to be found in the balance of those energies

Marie Moldovan

Marie Moldovan is a Saskatchewan native and Ontario immigrant. Some would call them a reverse snowbird, who feels most comfortable surrounded by snowcapped mountains.

Nomadic by nature, Marie is multifaceted and has mastered many skills. They dub themselves a jack of many trades and master of some. However, because Marie has acquired a plethora of diplomas spanning the educational spectrum, Marie's mother on the contrary would call them a professional student.

Marie would accredit their adaptability to the training they received as a Canadian Forces medic, and their artistic ability to their family. Both attributes have aided her along their journey from the points of homelessness and despair to the place of stability and optimism Marie has arrived at today.

In 2018, Marie was diagnosed with service-related PTSD, and within the same breath of time became a widow.

Unresolved trauma, and the loss of their husband caused Marie to skirt the edges of insanity. Faced with losing complete touch with reality, they returned to writing and art.

In a sense writing and art saved Marie's life, at least that's their claim. Fortunately, for the world, Marie's choice to embrace creation has led them to captain a new life as a publisher, illustrator, writer and artist.

Marie is the author of **20 years of Winter, Miss Sally Anne** and has currently opened the doors of her own publication organization, aptly named, **I Ain't Your Marionette Press**.

20 Years of Winter is an autobiographical collection of poetry and art. She published it in hopes to make a way for others who have suffered similar traumas to feel safe knowing that they are not alone nor are they to blame for their experiences. *20 Years of Winter* is Marie's source of empowerment offered to those victims to stand up to their perpetrators and to speak out against victim shaming.

ABOUT THE PUBLISHER

Alas, who are we, marionettes on strings? And what do we stand for, puppeteers of our destiny?

I Ain't Your Marionette distinguishes itself as a stronghold of artistic liberation. At its helm, Marie Moldovan, once a marionette of circumstance, now orchestrates a symphony of narrative freedom. The company's sanctuary breathes life into marionette authors, whose tales of resilience and aspiration paint a vivid tableau of human spirit.

82

The press's hallmark anthologies, **Shattered Psyche** and **The Way of The Crow**, are more than mere collections; they are immersive experiences that beckon readers to venture beyond the mundane. Each story or visual masterpiece is a declaration of independence, a narrative that defies the norm and invites a reimagining of the world.

The **Voces Animarum** exhibition, alongside the **Shattered Psyche Traveling Showcase** and **Colours of Collaboration**, exemplifies the press's dedication to breaking new ground in literary and artistic expression. These ventures not only elevate the company's stature but also reverberate through the artistic community.

FURTHER READING

***

Dive deeper into the captivating worlds crafted by Rick Powell. Each story in this collection explores the boundaries of love, loss, and the supernatural, inviting readers to confront their deepest fears and desires. Whether you're drawn to tales of obsession, apocalyptic nightmares, or chilling mysteries, there's something here for every lover of dark fiction.

Two Lost Souls:

Love, like life, is one of the oldest mysteries. But what happens when love turns into an obsession? When the boundaries between passion and madness blur, and the veil between the supernatural and natural world is cast aside? David believed his bond with his wife Helen was unbreakable, forged in the fires of life's trials. Yet, even the strongest love can be tested by the shadows that lurk in the corners of our hearts—and the darkness of a graveyard.

A Day of Ochre, Ascending:

In this apocalyptic nightmare inspired by Robert W. Chambers' The King in Yellow, a man's ordinary stroll with his dog turns into a nightmare. Each step plunges Walter and Archie deeper into a world of whispered doom. Will they escape, or will the nightmare consume them?

A Banquet of Panacea:

The loss of a child is a wound that never heals. But what if there was a way to move forward, a method so unthinkable it's only whispered about in the shadows? The Richards are living every parent's worst nightmare, their child's life stolen by a remorseless killer. In their darkest hour, they encounter Zhang, a billionaire with a chilling solution: when the justice system fails, he invites the families to a dinner shrouded in mystery and darkness.

Harold:

Frank is a seasoned detective with an uncanny 'feel' for things—a gift that has often guided him through the toughest cases. But this gift comes at a steep price. After years of risking his family and marriage for the job, Frank longs to slow down and reconnect with his loved ones. However, fate has other plans. A mysterious journal lands in his hands, chronicling the twisted crimes of a madman named Harold. Is this a work of fiction, or a chilling true-life account of a delusional killer?

Winston:

Julie lives with her mother in a rundown part of town, struggling to adjust to her mom's new boyfriend, a man she distrusts for many reasons. During a fateful walk home, she encounters Winston, an enigmatic old man whose presence is as captivating as it is mysterious. As their bond deepens, Julie's life begins to change in unimaginable ways. Who is Winston, and what secrets does he hold that could lift Julie out of her adversity? Is he a savior, or a messenger of doom?

Ornament:

The holidays are a time for gathering with friends, family, and loved ones.

Blazing fireplaces warm the bodies and hearts of those closest to us, as we share anecdotes of the year's events while the snow and bitter cold blow outside. But for Judith, the cold seeps inside her home, reflecting the turmoil in her life with John. Lies, cheating, and psychological abuse overshadow the season's joy, leaving her without a solution in sight.

Messages:

In a world where technology races forward, leaving yesterday's marvels in the dust, what if someone dared to blend ancient secrets with modern innovations? "Messages" delves into this terrifying possibility. Follow the harrowing journey of a reporter who uncovers the story of a lifetime—a story that could very well be his last. As he digs deeper, he finds himself trapped in a web of dark forces and apocalyptic realities.

A Glimpse Beyond the Veil:

The final book, *A Glimpse Beyond the Veil*, brings together all seven stories. Within this anthology of shadows, secrets writhe through the corridors of forgotten places and sinister whispers shroud the night. Each tale lures readers into the abyss to confront their deepest fears. This collection is a haunting exploration of the human condition and beckons readers to step into a world where reality blurs with the supernatural.

Thank
you for
your
support.